Zadie's Big Day

Martyn Hobbs

HELBLING LANGUAGES

www.helblinglanguages.com

Zadie's Big Day
by Martyn Hobbs

First published 2009

ISBN 978-3-85272-118-7

Series editor Maria Cleary
Activities by Elspeth Rawstron
Illustrated by Lorenzo Sabbatini
Design and layout by Pixarte
Printed by Athesia

About this Book

For the Student

Listen to the story and do some activities on your Audio CD

Talk about the story

beat• When you see the blue dot you can check the word in the glossary on pages 62-64

For the Teacher

Go to our Readers Resource site for information on using readers and downloadable Resource Sheets, photocopiable Worksheets, Answer Keys and Tapescripts. Plus the full version of the story on MP3.
www.helblingreaders.com

For lots of great ideas on using Graded Readers consult Reading Matters, the Teacher's Guide to using Helbling Readers.

Level 1 Structures

Present simple of *be*	*A / an*
Have got	*The*
There is / there are	Subject pronouns
Present Simple	Object pronouns
Can (ability and permission)	Plural nouns
Present continuous	Countable and uncountable nouns
	Some / any
Like / love / hate / don't like doing	
Imperatives	Adjectives
Short answers	Possessive adjectives
Who? What? Where? What colour?	Possessive *'s*
How much? How many?	Demonstrative adjectives and pronouns
Adverbs of frequency	*very*

Contents

Hi, I'm Zadie.
This is my story.
I love sports. Look through the book.
Can you guess my favourite sports?

Before Reading

1 Look at the picture and answer the questions on pages 8 and 9.

The Football Pitch

9
10
11
12
13
The Skate Park

Before Reading

1 **Label the football pitch with the words below.**

a) to kick b) to text c) to clap d) to cheer
e) to wag f) whistle g) referee h) goalkeeper

2 **Label the skate park with the words below.**

a) skateboard b) ramp c) helmet
d) body armour e) in-line skates

3 **The places in the pictures are important to the story. Why are they important? Can you guess? In groups write a scenario about one of the places. Include all the words in Exercise 1 or Exercise 2. Then tell the class. Choose the best scenario.**

4 **Talk about the picture.**

Which activity do you prefer?
Do you play for a football team?
Is there a girls' football team at your school?
Do you go skateboarding?
Are some sports 'just for girls' and other sports 'just for boys'?

5 What do the text messages say? Match.

a) ☐ Where R U?
b) ☐ CU 2MORO M8.
c) ☐ R U SOS?
d) ☐ Y R U L8?

1 Are you in trouble?
2 Why are you late?
3 See you tomorrow, mate•.
4 Where are you?

6 Listen and write the numbers that correspond to the names of each of the characters.

a) 

b) 

c) 

d) 

e) 

7 Answer the questions about you.

a) Which sports are you good at?

....

b) Which sports do you like doing?

....

c) Which sports do you like watching?

....

d) Do you prefer team sports or individual sports?

....

It's a cold wet afternoon in April.

It's a perfect day for sitting in a warm classroom, sending text messages to friends and looking out of the window. It's a perfect day for sitting in a warm office, sending emails and surfing• the net. It's a perfect day for looking for new clothes in the warm shopping centre. Or for sitting at home, drinking hot chocolate and watching afternoon TV.

But on the sports field of Westbourne High School, two football teams are running up and down, kicking• a heavy• wet football. It's an important match – the semi-final of the girls' football championship• between Westbourne and New Milton.

THWACK!

The goalkeeper kicks the football high into the air.

The team in red shirts run up the pitch, the team in blue shirts run back.

A girl in a red shirt with black hair and brown eyes watches the ball carefully. She walks slowly into the centre circle.

BOING!

A girl in a blue shirt heads the ball. It flies up into the grey air.

BIFF!

The ball lands at the feet of the girl with black hair. She immediately starts running towards the blue team's goal.

'Go on Zadie!' her team-mates shout.

Zadie runs quickly. The girls from New Milton can't catch her.
But then in front of her, Zadie sees a tall girl in a blue shirt. She's big. She's fast. And she's right in front of her!
But Zadie has an idea.
Zadie kicks the ball to the girl's left, and then runs to the girl's right.
The tall girl is confused. She looks at the ball, she looks at Zadie. She doesn't know which way to move. So Zadie runs past her, and gets the ball on the other side!
Now she has only the goalkeeper to beat.

The goalkeeper waves• her arms and opens her legs, ready to jump in any direction. But Zadie has a better idea.
THUMP!
She kicks the ball between the goalkeeper's legs into the back of the New Milton net.
'Goal!!!'
Holly, Grace and her other team-mates run up to Zadie, smiling happily. The score is 1-0 to Westbourne. And there are only another fifteen minutes to play.
The game is nearly over.
But now Zadie is having fun.

With twelve minutes to play, Zadie jumps into the air and kicks the ball over her head. It's her famous scissor kick! The ball shoots• into the back of the New Milton goal.
CRASH!

With five minutes to play, Zadie crosses• the ball to Grace who heads it past the goalkeeper.
BANG!

And in the last minute of the match, Zadie stops the ball with her chest, turns to her left, then kicks the ball with all her power. It goes like a rocket into the New Milton net.
WALLOP!

The referee• blows her whistle•. It's the end of the game. Westbourne are in the final!

Once again, Zadie is the hero.
The Westbourne players walk happily off the pitch towards the changing room. A smiling woman with short red hair walks over to Zadie. It's Petty the Pirate.
Actually, her real name is Karen Petty. She's their sports teacher. But because she has a small tattoo on her wrist, all the students call her Petty the Pirate – but not to her face!
'Great game, Zadie,' she says.
'Thanks, Ms Petty,' Zadie replies.
'The final is in two weeks against Greenford. They're a really tough• team.'
'Don't worry, miss. We can win!'
And Zadie gives a big confident• smile.

At home, Zadie doesn't feel like a hero.

First of all, there's her brother Eric. Now Eric is fifteen years old and clever. In fact, he's very clever.

'Eric has his exam results,' says her dad, as Zadie walks into the kitchen. Her father is making dinner because her mother works late on Wednesdays at the hospital. Eric gives Zadie a little smile. He looks a bit embarrassed.

'Oh really?' she says.

'Yes, he's top in• history, English, science and maths.'

Zadie's father thinks that exam results are very, very important.

'That's good,' says Zadie.

'Good? It's excellent! You know, it's very important to do well at school... and your results aren't very good.'

Zadie nods•.
She doesn't like sitting in a classroom all day looking at books. And she hates taking exams. She can't remember all those stupid facts! But Eric is brilliant at exams. He can remember everything.
'Tell me about the game,' says Eric.
'We're in the final.'
'Fantastic!' Eric is always impressed by• Zadie. He is hopeless• at sport.
'How many goals?'
'Three for me, four for the team.'
'Amazing!'
Her father doesn't hear this conversation. He is busy cooking. He empties a jar of pasta sauce into a pan and then looks round.
'Don't forget to do your homework tonight, Zadie. Oh, and after dinner, can you babysit• Tania?'

Zadie's second problem at home is Tania, her kid sister•.
Tania is five. And whenever• her parents need a babysitter, Zadie is always the person they think of first.
'Oh, dad, why can't Eric do it?'
'Sorry, Zadie,' says Eric. 'I'm going out.'
'But I want to go out, too!' says Zadie.
'You can go out after dinner,' says her father, 'and take the dog for a walk. Then you have to look after your sister.'
'That is so unfair•!'
Zadie turns round and walks out of the kitchen.
'Come back and lay• the table!' her father shouts after her.
'Your dinner's ready!'

Her third problem is their dog, Scamp. Eric never takes him for a walk. It's always Zadie.

Actually, that isn't a problem. Zadie likes taking Scamp out for a run. It's a good excuse for her to go in-line skating. So after dinner, Zadie puts on her new red top, new blue earrings, her skates and finally her MP3 player – and she's ready to go!

Scamp wags• his tail and gives a little bark•. He's ready to go, too.

'Don't be long,' her dad says, doing the washing-up•.

But Zadie is already out of the door and on her way.

She skates through the park, under the trees with their new green leaves. The rain is over and the sun is shining. There's a wonderful smell of spring in the air. Zadie loves this time of year. It always promises adventure. She dreams of going on a dangerous expedition• up the river Amazon, or skydiving• from a plane, or hang-gliding• over the sea, or white-water rafting• in the Rocky Mountains... but she's too young. And her parents always tell her to think about school. To study. To do her homework. To forget her wild ideas. Life is so unfair!
So Zadie skates quickly through the park... while Scamp tries to stay by her side!

Zadie sees Grace at the skate park. She goes over to her.
'Hi Grace.'
'Hi Zadie. I like your earrings.'
'Thanks,' Zadie says.
Then Grace pats• Scamp on the head. He licks• her hand. He likes Grace.
Zadie looks at a boy with a skateboard. He has got lots of friends with him.
'Who's that?' asks Zadie.
'His name's Simon. He's new at school. He's in the year above us.'
Zadie remembers him.
'What's going on?' she asks.
'He's doing some tricks,' Grace replies. 'He's really good.'
At that moment, Simon gets on his skateboard and moves towards a ramp...

'He's good-looking, isn't he?' says Grace.
Zadie gives her a look.
'Grace, you like every boy in school!'
'No, I don't!' But Grace laughs and her face goes a bit red.

Simon goes quickly up a ramp, turns, and then shoots down again. He is moving very fast. Then he goes up another ramp and shoots up into the air.

When he lands on the back two wheels of his skateboard, all his friends cheer•. Grace claps• her hands.

'He's fantastic!' Grace says.

'He's OK,' says Zadie. She isn't impressed by this new boy. Her friends call her 'The Queen of the Skate Park'. And she always wants to be number one.

4
I can show Simon some tricks, too.
Hey, Zadie, you're not wearing your helmet.
Don't worry about me. Just watch.

So Zadie skates past Simon and goes up the ramp.
It's my turn now.

Zadie turns once, twice...
Three times in the air!
Then she lands and comes to a perfect stop.

Zadie skates over to Grace. Scamp jumps up at her and wags his tail.

'So, what do you think?' asks Zadie.

'Brilliant!' says Grace, smiling.

They look over at the boys. They are talking quietly to each other, not looking at the girls. Then Simon turns to them and says, 'Not a bad trick. What's your name?'

'Zadie.'

'OK, Zadie. See you around.'

Then the boys start going away.

'I have to go home now, too,' says Grace. 'It's getting late.'

Zadie looks at her watch. It's very late!

'See you tomorrow!' says Zadie.

'Yeah, bye!'

When Zadie gets home she is in big trouble.
'What time do you call this?' asks her father. He looks angry.
'I'm sorry, Dad.'
'Now go into the sitting room and stay with your sister.'
Her father gets his jacket, goes to the front door, and stops. Then he comes back and gives Zadie a kiss.
'Be good.'
'Yeah,' says Zadie.'
'See you later,' he says. 'And do your homework.'
Zadie tries to write an essay• about The Great Fire of London in 1666 while her kid sister watches a DVD. After half an hour she sits on the sofa with Tania and they watch the film together. And after another half an hour they are both asleep.

A few days later, Zadie is hanging out• with Holly and Grace in the school playground. She is playing them the new ringtone• on her mobile when her classmate Jack comes over. Jack never likes chatting to girls. So they know he has a special reason to talk to them. It only takes ten seconds to find out what it is.

'Hey, Zadie,' says Jack.
'Hi, Jack,' says Zadie. 'Is everything OK?'
'Sure,' says Jack. 'Do you know Simon?'
'I don't know him, but I know who he is.'
'Well, he wants to talk to you.'
'Cool,' says Zadie.
Jack gives a little smile, and then walks over to join his gang.

'What's that all about?' asks Holly.
'Maybe Simon fancies you,' says Grace.
'Ha ha, very funny,' says Zadie. And then she thinks, 'What does he want?'
But Simon doesn't speak to her that day.
And he doesn't speak to her on Tuesday.
On Wednesday morning she sees him as she is walking into the playground. She is carrying her sports bag with her football gear. Simon is talking to his friends. Simon sees her and then says something to them. They all laugh.
Zadie ignores them and goes straight into the school.
Sometimes boys make her really mad!

They have football practice after school.
Petty the Pirate talks to the team before they start.
'OK girls, the final's on Saturday. Greenford are a good team. They're strong. They're fast. And they play hard. But I'm sure you can win.'
'With Zadie in the team, we can beat anyone,' says Holly. And all her team-mates agree.
Zadie is a bit embarrassed, but she is looking forward• to the match. She loves football. And she loves winning.
'The final's at the local stadium. The kick-off• is at 10.30. Can you all get there by 10 o'clock?'
Everyone says 'yes'. And then they run onto the football pitch.

It's only a practice game, but Zadie plays as if it's the final. Her team win 10-6. Zadie scores five goals. Her last goal comes from a corner kick. Samira takes the corner and Zadie runs towards the goal then jumps. She flies through the air like a plane and heads the ball into the top of the net. She lands on her chest with a crash. Petty the Pirate rushes over to her.
'Are you all right?' she asks. She looks worried.
Zadie looks up at her from the ground. Her chest hurts•, but she smiles.
'Don't worry, miss. I'm fine.'
'Take it easy, Zadie. This is only a training session•.'
But Zadie never listens. She always gives 110%.

THUMP

By the time they leave school, a light rain is falling. Zadie, Holly and Grace are heading towards the school gates when Holly says, 'Look over there.' They see a group of boys waiting at the gates.

'Who are they?' asks Zadie.

'They look like Simon's friends,' says Grace.

'And there's Simon,' says Holly.

'I guess he wants to talk to me now,' says Zadie.

And she walks across the playground towards them.

As they approach the group, one of the boys says:

'Here they come. The girl footballers!'

The others laugh.

But Simon doesn't laugh. He just watches them.
Then as they are walking through the gates, Simon says:
'Hi.'
Zadie stops.
'Hi.'
'You're name's Zadie, isn't it?' he says.
'That's right.'
'I hear you're good at football.'
The boys laugh again.
'Maybe.'
'That's cool,' says Simon, and he looks at his mates. They don't laugh this time. Then he turns back to Zadie and her friends.
'You're pretty good on skates, too.'
'Thanks,' says Zadie.
'But you're not the best,' says Simon.

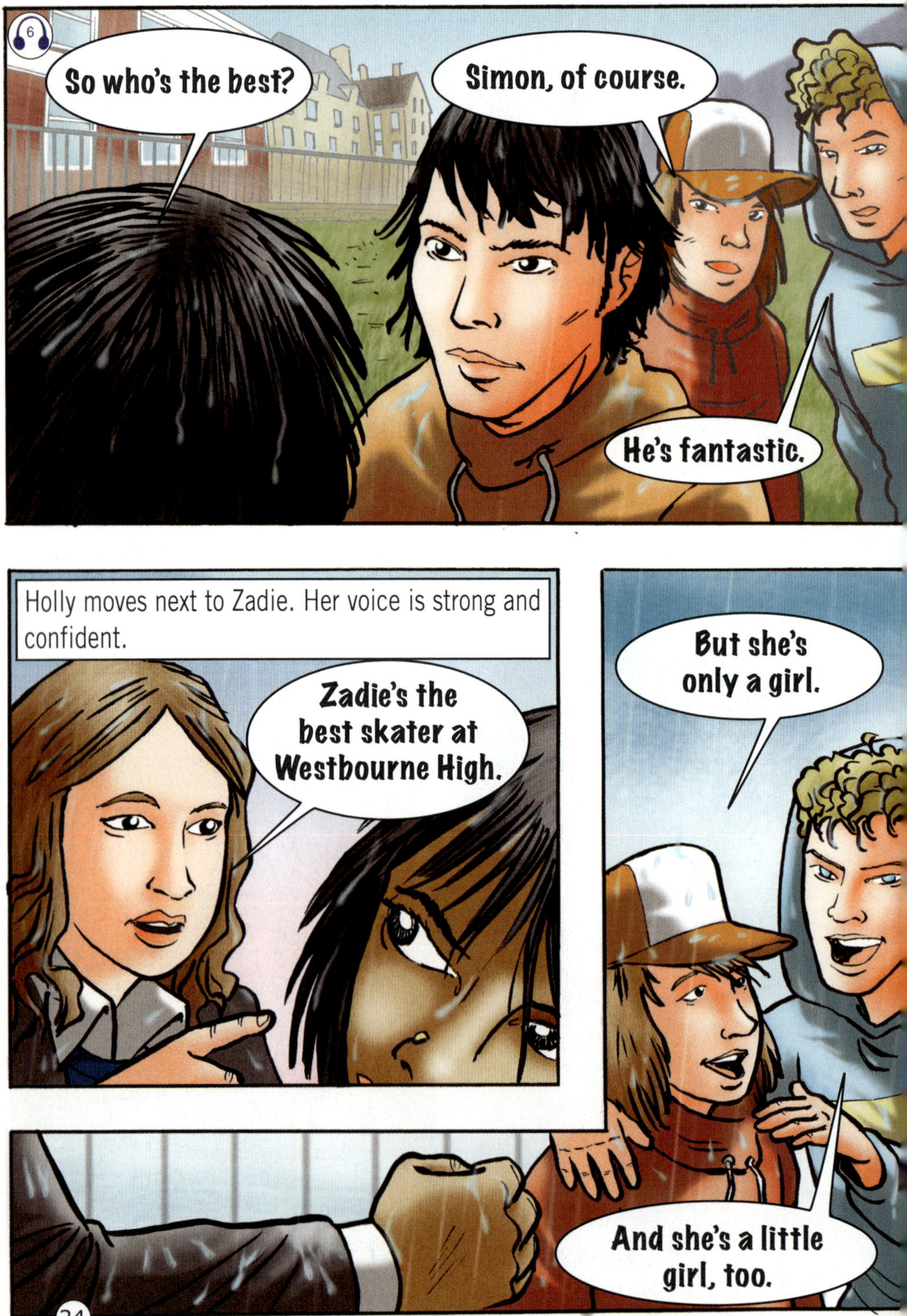
So who's the best?
Simon, of course.
He's fantastic.
Holly moves next to Zadie. Her voice is strong and confident.
Zadie's the best skater at Westbourne High.
But she's only a girl.
And she's a little girl, too.

That makes Zadie so angry she wants to explode.
OK then. Let's have a competition. I can prove I'm number one!
That's fine by me.
Good.
Skateboard or in-line skating?
I don't care. You choose.
Actually, Zadie prefers in-line skating. She doesn't go skateboarding anymore.
OK, skateboarding.
Cool.

It is raining quite heavily now.

'When do you want to meet?' asks Simon.

'Any time,' says Zadie.

'Saturday?'

'Fine.'

Holly interrupts•.

'Hey, Zadie. Don't forget. We've got the football final on Saturday.'

'What time's kick-off?' asks Simon.

'Half past ten,' Zadie replies.

'All right then. Let's meet in the morning. Say about half past eight?

'No worries,' says Zadie. 'See you then.'

Zadie gives Simon the thumbs up• and walks away with Holly and Grace.

Now Zadie can only think of one thing... and it isn't the football final. She has two days to practise on her skateboard, and it's already Wednesday, and it's getting late, and the weather's terrible.
As soon as she gets home she runs upstairs and looks for her skateboard.
It isn't in her room.
It isn't in the garden shed•.
And it isn't in the cupboard under the stairs.
'Zadie,' her mother asks. 'What are you looking for?'
Zadie looks out from the cupboard.
'My skateboard. Do you know where it is?'
Her mother smiles.
'Of course I do. It's with all your other old things.'

Zadie climbs up into the loft• and finds her old skateboard in a corner next to an old trunk•. She takes it downstairs.

'Dad,' she says as she walks into the kitchen. 'Have you got any oil?'

Her father looks up from his newspaper.

'Why do you need it?' he asks.

'I want to use my skateboard again.'

Then while her father is oiling her skateboard, Eric comes in.

'Hey, Zadie, I can take Scamp for a walk today,' he says.

Zadie looks surprised. Eric never takes Scamp out!

'You have to stay relaxed for the final,' he says.

But Zadie has to practise on her skateboard!

'Thanks, Eric, that's a really nice idea. But I can take Scamp for a walk. Really!'

So with her helmet, her body armour•, her skateboard and Scamp (of course!) Zadie steps out into the rain. Scamp runs happily down the road, barking and wagging his tail. Then he stops and looks around, confused.
Where's Zadie? She always skates along in front of him. Scamp looks back and sees her on the skateboard. She isn't having an easy time.
'This is terrible,' thinks Zadie. 'It feels really weird• using a skateboard again. But I have to be good on Saturday. I have to win!'
So she wipes• the rain from her face, and tries to go fast.

Zadie races along and turns at the corner. But the skateboard skids•
on the wet pavement. She loses her balance and...
CRASH!
The skateboard flies across the road and Zadie lands on her behind. She shakes her head. She feels OK (actually she feels a bit stupid) but there is a hole in the knee of her new jeans. And then she hears someone laughing. It's a boy's laugh. She looks up and sees Charlie, one of Simon's friends.
'Hey, it's Zadie, 'The Queen of the Skate Park'', he says.
Zadie looks the other way. She isn't smiling.
When she gets home her mother is very annoyed• about the hole in her jeans. And then her father says, 'Don't forget your homework, Zadie!'
Life is so unfair!

Zadie sees Simon and his friends during break• on Friday morning. He says:
'Hey, Zadie. I've got an idea.'
'What's that?'
'There's a new skate park on the other side of town. It has nice big ramps. Why don't we meet there?'
'Cool,' says Zadie.
Then Charlie says something about her and they all laugh.
As soon as she gets home, Zadie grabs her skateboard and goes out practising again. She only has one thought on her mind – and it isn't the football final. She tries some jumps and turns. This time she doesn't fall over. She knows she can win.

Zadie is having her breakfast on Saturday morning when her parents come into the kitchen.
'You're early, darling,' her mother says.
'I'm OK,' Zadie replies. 'I just want to do some extra training before the match.'
Her parents don't know anything about the skateboard competition.
'It's your big day today,' her father says, putting on the kettle•. 'Can we come and watch?'
They never watch her play football!
'I know it's an important game,' her father adds.
'That's fine,' Zadie says. She checks the time on her mobile and gets up. 'Well, I have to go now. See you later.'
'See you,' her mother says. 'And good luck.'
'I need luck,' thinks Zadie, 'but not for the football match!'

The new skateboard park is over half an hour away. But when she arrives, the place is deserted. So she walks around and looks at the ramps. Simon is right. They are very high.

Simon and his friends don't arrive until after nine o'clock.

'You're late,' Zadie says.

Simon shrugs.

'Are you ready to lose?' he asks.

'I never lose,' Zadie says. 'So what are we waiting for? Let's start.'

They take it in turns to do their jumps.

They are both very good.

And they both make no mistakes.

Simon's friends watch them carefully.

They aren't laughing now.

They can see Zadie is very talented.

8
OK, Zadie.
Let's get serious.
Watch this.
Simon speeds• down one ramp
... up another ramp... and shoots into the air.
He turns twice...
... and lands safely!

Two turns is nothing. I can do three.
Take it easy, Zadie.
Don't worry about me.

So this time Zadie shoots up like a rocket into the air...
She turns once... twice... three times!

But when she hits the ground the skateboard spins• away.
And Zadie falls off and lands on her arm.
'OUCH!'
Simon immediately runs to her side.
'Are you all right, Zadie?' he asks. He is very worried.
'It's my arm,' says Zadie.
'Let me take a look,' he says. He carefully pulls up her shirt. Her arm is bleeding•. Then they hear a noise.
'What's that?'
'It's my mobile,' says Zadie. 'Can you get it?'
Her mobile phone is lying on the ground nearby. Simon passes it to her and Zadie opens the text message. It's from Grace:

Y R U L8?
Where R U?

Zadie starts crying.
'I am *so* stupid,' she says.
'No, you aren't,' says Simon. 'You're a brilliant skateboarder.'
'But my arm really hurts, and it's getting late. The football final starts in half an hour.'
'Don't worry, I can get you to the match on time,' says Simon.
'How?'
'On my bike. Come on.'
So Zadie sits on the crossbar• of the bike, Simon sits on the seat.
'OK?' he asks.
'Fine,' Zadie replies.
'Now this time,' Simon says with a smile, 'don't fall off!'
They set off for the sports stadium with his friends following behind.

They arrive at twenty past ten. Petty the Pirate runs up to them.
'I'm sorry I'm late,' says Zadie. 'I can explain later.'

'Put on your football gear,' says Petty the Pirate.

'Thanks, Simon!' says Zadie, then she runs into the changing room, holding her bad arm.

'Good luck!' shouts Simon.

The match starts badly. The Greenford team are strong. After five minutes, Zadie jumps for a ball and a Greenford player pushes• her in the back. She lands with a thump• and cries out in pain.

Then soon after, Zadie tries to take a throw-in. But when she throws the ball, her arm hurts very badly, and the ball rolls to a Greenford player.

Zadie's team-mates are worried.

'Are you all right?' Holly asks.

Zadie shakes her head unhappily.

Her father turns to Eric in the crowd.

'What's wrong with Zadie?' he asks.

'I don't know, Dad. She never plays like this.'

The match doesn't get any better for Westbourne. After twenty minutes, Greenford score their first goal. And after twenty-five minutes, they score their second. 2–0! Zadie finds it difficult to run. She isn't playing well. Then the referee blows her whistle. It's half-time.

In the changing room, Petty the Pirate examines• Zadie's arm.
'This looks bad,' she says. 'I don't think you can play.'
'Oh, please, Ms Petty,' says Zadie. 'Please. I have to play.'
Petty the Pirate thinks for a long time. Then she sprays Zadie's arm and puts a bandage around it.

'OK, Zadie. But be careful. You can't play your usual physical game. So use your intelligence.'

The second half is similar to the first. But at least Greenford don't get another goal.
Then with fifteen minutes to go, Zadie gets the ball.
Think, Zadie, think!
THWACK!
GOAL!!!

With five minutes to go, Grace kicks the ball. Zadie jumps over it, and...
GOAL!!!
Then in the last minute, Westbourne get a corner.
This is no time to be careful!
Penalty!
BIFF!

11 It is the last kick of the match. Zadie is holding her arm in pain.
'Can you take the penalty?' asks Grace.
Zadie nods. She is trying not to cry again.
She puts the ball on the penalty spot and looks at the goalkeeper.
'Come on, Zadie,' shouts Simon.
Her parents, Eric and Tania don't say a word. They are too nervous!
Zadie runs up to the ball, looking to her left. But she kicks the ball to her right and the goalkeeper dives• the wrong way. The ball rolls slowly into the Greenford goal. The referee blows her whistle for the last time. Westbourne are the champions!

Zadie is the hero of the day.
Petty the Pirate says, 'A fantastic game, Zadie! Fantastic!'
Simon says, 'You're the best footballer, Zadie, and the best skateboarder!'
And her father says, 'You're so clever, Zadie! You're brilliant.'
When she gets home, Zadie throws her skateboard into the loft. She doesn't want to use it again! And she's so tired, she doesn't take Scamp for a walk. She has a bath and goes to bed early.
But her adventures aren't over yet.
That night, she dreams of snowboarding down Mount Everest.
And in the morning, she wakes up with a new ambition•.

After Reading

Understanding the story

1 **Match the sentences to the characters. Write the names.**

Zadie Jack Grace Ms Petty Simon Eric

a) .... is hopeless at sport.

b) .... likes every boy in school.

c) .... doesn't like chatting to girls.

d) .... is a new boy at school.

e) .... has got a tattoo on her wrist.

f) .... always wants to be number one.

2 **Why are the following characters important to the story? Discuss with a partner.**

a) Zadie
b) Ms Petty
c) Simon
d) Grace

3 Read the sentences then choose the correct word or words for each space.

a) Zadie is the hero of the girls' ....
1 in-line skating team   2 skateboarding team   3 football team

b) Zadie's brother is no good at sport but he's very ....
1 clever   2 confident   3 friendly

c) In the park, Zadie watches Simon ....
1 doing some tricks   2 playing football   3 in-line skating

d) There is a practice game before the final. Zadie scores .... goals.
1 four   2 three   3 five

e) Zadie hurts her arm in the ....
1 changing room   2 football match   3 skateboarding competition

f) .... dives the wrong way and Zadie scores a goal. Westbourne wins the match.
1 The referee   2 The goalkeeper   3 Holly

4 Read the summary of the story and correct the mistakes.

Zadie loves sport. She is the best player on the school hockey team and she is also the best skateboarder at Westbourne High. One day, in the centre of town, she meets Eric, a new boy at school. Eric is a good skateboarder. He and Zadie decide to have a competition to decide who is best. The competition is on the day of an important football final. Zadie doesn't practise her skateboarding. On her big day she hurts herself at the competition and she misses the football final. Westbourne High lose and her team-mates are angry with her.

After Reading

Vocabulary

1 **Match the actions with the pictures.**

a) 

b) 

c) 

d) 

1 to bleed 2 to head 3 to text 4 to land

2 **Write a description of each picture.**

a) ....

b) ....

c) ....

d) ....

3 **Look at the pictures and ask and answer questions with a partner.**

What's the matter with Zadie in the last picture?

4 Complete the speech bubbles with the adjectives in the box below.

big bad good-looking mad tough

5 When can you use these phrases? Match.

a) ☐ See you around.
b) ☐ Take it easy.
c) ☐ What time do you call this?
d) ☐ Let's get serious.

1 When you need to do something.
2 Somebody is late.
3 You are saying goodbye to somebody.
4 You want somebody to be careful.

6 Now find the phrases in the story. Who says them? Write their names below.

a) .... b) ....

c) .... d) ....

After Reading
Grammar

Practise the Present Continuous.

1 Look at the pictures. What is happening? Write a sentence about each picture with the verbs below.

skid pat shoot skate dive blow

a) 

....

b) 

....

c) 

....

d) 

....

e) 

....

f) 

....

Practise the Present Simple.

2 Fill in the blanks with the correct form of the verbs in the box.

be	decide	feel	go	take	think

a) Zadie .... the best player on her team.
b) At home Zadie .... like a hero.
c) Zadie's father .... that exam results are very important.
d) Zadie and Simon .... to have a skateboard competition.
e) Zadie .... skateboarding any more.
f) At the end Simon .... Zadie to the stadium on his bike.

Practise asking questions.

3 You are interviewing Zadie for the school magazine.

You: .... ?
Zadie: My name's Zadie.
You: .... ?
Zadie: I go to Westbourne High School.
You: .... ?
Zadie: My favourite sport is football.
You: .... ?
Zadie: I play for Westbourne. It's our school team.
You: .... ?
Zadie: Our team colour is red.
You: .... ?
Zadie: Yes, I've got a brother and a sister.
You: .... ?
Zadie: No, my brother doesn't play football.
You: .... ?
Zadie: No, it isn't a boy's game. Girls can play football just as well as boys.
You: Thank you, Zadie. Good luck for Saturday.
Zadie: Thanks.

After Reading

Test

12 **1 Listen to the conversations and choose the correct picture.**

a) 1 ☐ 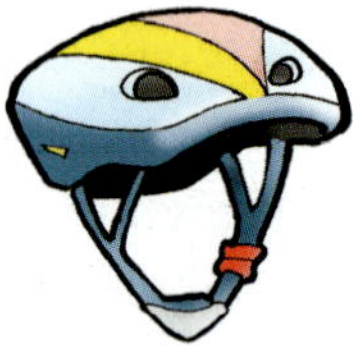 2 ☐  3 ☐ 

b) 1 ☐  2 ☐  3 ☐ 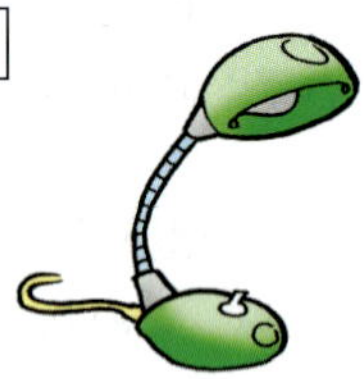

c) 1 ☐  2 ☐  3 ☐ 

d) 1 ☐ 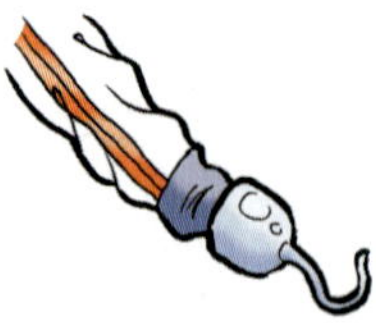 2 ☐ 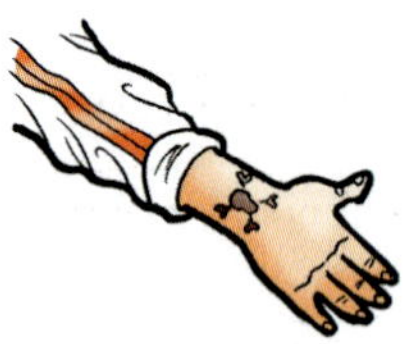 3 ☐ 

e) 1 ☐  2 ☐  3 ☐ 

2 **Read the sentences about the story and choose the best word (1, 2 or 3) for each space.**

a) Zadie is in the girls' .... team.
1 football   2 volleyball   3 basketball

b) Eric is top of the class in ....
1 geography   2 maths   3 music

c) Zadie is .... her team can win the championship.
1 confident   2 confused   3 embarrassed

d) Simon is .... Zadie's skating.
1 upset by   2 interrupted by   3 impressed by

e) **Zadie:** What time does the match start?
Ms Petty: The .... at 10.30.
1 kick-off's   2 whistle's   3 throw-in's

3 **Write a commentary for a football match. Use the words below.**

champions dive kick head goalkeeper score goal

Today's match is (name of team) .... against (name of team) ....

(name of team) .... are winning. The score is ....

(name of player) .... has got the ball now. S/he is .... it to (name of player) ....

....

....

Glossary

9 **mate:** friend
11 **championship:** competition
heavy: that weighs a lot; not light
kicking: hitting with your foot
surfing the net: looking at Internet sites
12 **heads:** hits with her head
lands: comes to the ground
pitch: football field
team-mates: people in the same team
13 **beat:** win against
right: exactly; directly
14 **crosses:** kicks across
referee: person who controls a match
shoots: goes quickly
waves: moves from side to side
whistle: small metal tube that makes a high sound when you blow into it
16 **confident:** sure of what she says
tough: hard
17 **top in:** first in the class
19 **babysit:** look after a young child
hopeless: very bad
impressed by: he thinks she is great
kid sister: younger sister
lay: put plates, etc. on a table before a meal
nods: moves her head up and down to say 'yes'
unfair: not right
whenever: when
20 **bark:** sound a dog makes
wags: when a dog moves its tail from side to side
washing-up: cleaning plates, etc. after a meal
21 **expedition:** adventurous journey
hang-gliding: flying a light plane without a motor (hang-glider)
skydiving: jumping from a plane with a parachute
white-water rafting: going down very fast rivers in a small boat (raft)

22 **licks:** touches with his tongue
pats: touches gently with her hand
23 **cheer:** shout loudly to show they like what he is doing
claps: hits her hands together to show she likes what he is doing
27 **essay:** piece of writing
28 **hanging out:** being with your friends
ringtone: sound of a phone when it rings
29 **fancies:** likes in a romantic way
gear: clothes for a sport
mad: angry
30 **kick-off:** start of a football match
hurts: is sore; has a pain
looking forward: happy about something in the future
training session: time when you practise a sport
32 **approach:** come close to
35 **prove:** show; make clear and evident
that's fine by me: I think that's OK
36 **interrupts:** stops her from talking
thumbs up: sign to say 'ok'
37 **shed:** small building where you keep things
38 **loft:** room in the roof space; attic
trunk: a large box or case
39 **body armour:** protection for head, knees, elbows and wrists
weird: strange
wipes: cleans; dries; takes away
40 **annoyed:** angry; cross
skids: slides/moves without control
41 **break:** free time between lessons at school
42 **kettle:** where you boil water
43 **deserted:** empty
shrugs: raises his shoulders to say he is not interested
talented: with natural ability
44 **speeds:** moves fast
46 **bleeding:** she is losing blood from a cut
spins: moves in circles
47 **crossbar:** bar across the top of a bike
48 **pushes:** moves with force with her hands
with a thump: hard; heavily

49 **examines:** checks; looks at carefully
50 **similar:** like; the same
to go: before the finish
51 **penalty:** kick in front of the goal
52 **dives:** jumps
53 **ambition:** something you want to do